MARVEL
SPIDER-MAN

THE VULTURE

This edition published by Parragon Books Ltd in 2014

Parragon Books Ltd
Chartist House
15–17 Trim Street
Bath BA1 1HA, UK
www.parragon.com

marvel.com

© 2014 MARVEL

Writer: Joe Caramagna
Comic Artists: Francesca Ciregia & Elena Casagrande
Colourist: Sotocolor
Letterer: Joe Caramagna
Cover Artists: Patrick Scherberger with Edgar Delgado
Spot Illustrations: Scott Koblish with Sotocolor and Paul Ryan, John Romita
& Damion Scott
Assistant Editor: Michael Horwitz
Comic Editors: Nathan Cosby & Jordan D. White
Prose Editor: Cory Levine

ISBN 978-1-4723-4215-7

Printed in China

THE VULTURE

Bath · New York · Cologne · Melbourne · Delhi
Hong Kong · Shenzhen · Singapore · Amsterdam

SPIDER-MAN

THE FORMER PROFESSIONAL WRESTLER TURNED SUPER HERO LEARNED THE HARD WAY THAT WITH GREAT POWER MUST COME GREAT RESPONSIBILITY. TO MAKE UP FOR HIS PAST MISTAKES, HE HAS VOWED TO PROTECT NEW YORK CITY FROM ALL THOSE WHO WISH TO DO HARM.

PETER PARKER

RAISED BY HIS UNCLE BEN AND AUNT MAY, HE ALWAYS DREAMED OF BECOMING A SCIENTIST LIKE HIS LATE FATHER. BUT AFTER A LAB ACCIDENT — AND A RADIOACTIVE SPIDER BITE — GRANTS HIM SPECIAL POWERS, HE DISCOVERS HIS TRUE CALLING.

UNCLE BEN

As Peter's father figure, Uncle Ben has taught him many life lessons. But the most important one of all is that 'with great power there must also come great responsibility'.

AUNT MAY

After the death of Peter's parents, May Parker and her husband, Ben, raised their nephew as if he were their own child.

FLASH THOMPSON

Eugene 'Flash' Thompson is Midtown High's star football player but also its biggest bully. Little does he know his favourite victim, Peter Parker, is really New York City's greatest super hero!

J. JONAH JAMESON

THE PUBLISHER OF THE *DAILY BUGLE* BRINGS ATTENTION TO HIS FLOUNDERING NEWSPAPER BY GOING AFTER NEW YORK CITY'S BELOVED COSTUMED VIGILANTE.

CAPTAIN STACY

AS A VETERAN OF THE POLICE DEPARTMENT, CAPTAIN STACY KEEPS LAW AND ORDER IN NEW YORK CITY.

THE VULTURE

ADRIAN TOOMES SPENT HIS LIFE AS AN ENGINEER BUT NEVER FELT APPRECIATED BY HIS EMPLOYERS. AFTER HE WAS FIRED, HE DECIDED TO USE HIS GREATEST INVENTION, THE VULTURE HARNESS, TO GAIN THE RESPECT HE FELT HE HAD ALWAYS DESERVED.

SANDMAN

WHILE HE WAS ON THE RUN FROM THE POLICE, A CHEMICAL ACCIDENT LEFT CRIMINAL FLINT MARKO WITH THE ABILITY TO TURN HIS BODY INTO SAND.

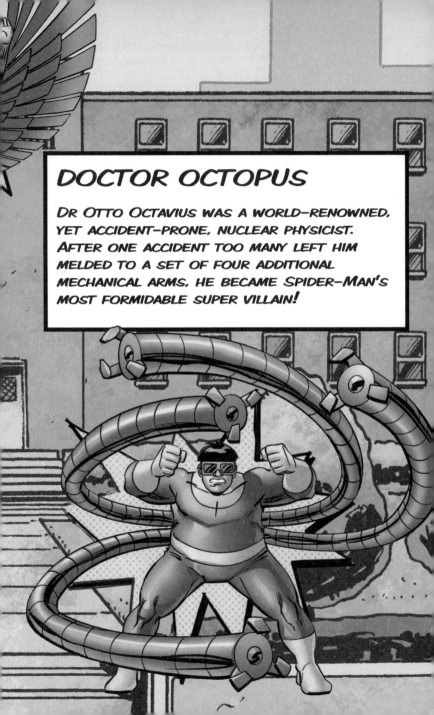

DOCTOR OCTOPUS

DR OTTO OCTAVIUS WAS A WORLD-RENOWNED, YET ACCIDENT-PRONE, NUCLEAR PHYSICIST. AFTER ONE ACCIDENT TOO MANY LEFT HIM MELDED TO A SET OF FOUR ADDITIONAL MECHANICAL ARMS, HE BECAME SPIDER-MAN'S MOST FORMIDABLE SUPER VILLAIN!

GREEN GOBLIN

NORMAN OSBORN IS A MILITARY CONTRACTOR WHO WAS TASKED WITH DEVELOPING A SUPER-SOLDIER SERUM. BUT, ASIDE FROM EXTRAORDINARY ABILITIES, HIS FLAWED FORMULA ALSO BRINGS OUT HIS DEVILISH DARK SIDE!

KRAVEN THE HUNTER

AFTER CONQUERING THE FIERCEST ANIMALS IN ALL THE JUNGLES OF AFRICA, THE HUNTER SERGEI KRAVINOFF SETS HIS SIGHTS ON THE MOST ELUSIVE PREY OF THEM ALL, SPIDER-MAN!

THE LIZARD

DR CURT CONNORS DEVELOPED A SERUM TO REPLICATE IN HUMANS A LIZARD'S ABILITY TO REGENERATE LIMBS. BUT WHEN HE TESTS IT ON HIMSELF, HE GETS MORE THAN HE BARGAINED FOR!

CHAPTER
1

The tourists on their way to the
Broadway matinees got a greater show than
they bargained for that day! Theatregoers
dived in all directions when the purple
car skidded round the corner on two

wheels before cutting into the midday traffic on 7th Avenue. Inside the car, three girls in French street mime costumes calling themselves Pinky, Binky and Sue shrieked loudly as the distant sound of police sirens drew closer.

SKREEEE!

Pinky pushed down on the accelerator. As the car lurched forward, she checked the rear-view mirror to see if he was still there.

"Are you sure that's him?" Binky asked. "Isn't he supposed to have eight arms or something?"

"Who else could he be?" Pinky asked. "He's webbed to our bumper!" Sue looked out of the rear windscreen. Sure enough, he was still there: the skinny guy in the red and blue costume the papers were calling Spider-Man!

But Spider-Man wasn't very happy to be there, either. It seemed like whenever there was a choice to be made, he made the wrong one.

It all started a couple of weeks ago when, while on a class trip, Peter Parker was bitten by a radioactive spider – and developed the proportional strength and abilities of the arachnid. But instead of using his new powers to do good deeds, he first used them to try to become rich and famous. Then one night when he had the chance to stop a burglar, he chose to let him get away, instead.

Later that night, the same burglar broke into his house and shot his Uncle Ben. Because of his bad choices, he

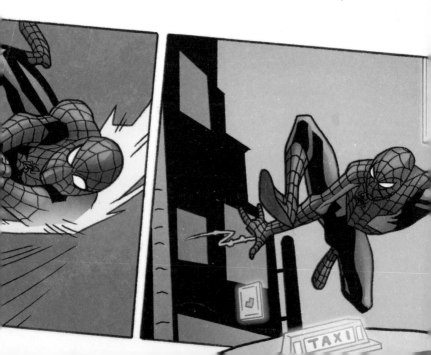

learned that with great power, there must also come great responsibility. Ever since, he's been known as Spider-Man, New York City's newest super hero crime fighter!

When Pinky, Binky and Sue ran from the bank with large bags of money in their hands and got into their getaway car, Spider-Man could have stopped them in many different ways. He chose what he thought was the easiest way and shot a web to the bumper of the car to keep it from driving away. Normally, that would have worked, thanks to his super-strength.

But as the car
zoomed away,
Spider-Man was
caught off-balance,
yanked right off
his feet and
dragged through
midtown
Manhattan!

As he was
pulled across
the tarmac,
Spider-Man tried
to get to his feet.
*If I dig my heels
in, I might be able
to stand ... like a water skier!* he thought.
But when he sat up, he felt the rough city
street chewing up the seat of his trousers!
If he wanted to keep his costume on (and
in one piece) he had to come up with a
better plan.

He let go of the web with one hand.
As he zoomed through the next junction,
he aimed his wrist and pressed a small

button in the palm of his hand. With a THWIP!, a web fired from the web-shooter bracelet hidden beneath his costume and stuck to the thick base of a passing lamppost!

With one web on the car and another on the lamppost, Spider-Man pulled them both with all his might. Searing pain shot all the way up to his shoulders. The spinning wheels of the purple car screeched as it veered across two lanes of traffic.

It bounced up on the kerb, across the pavement and right through the glass front of an Italian restaurant with a loud SMASH! It worked!

A police car with flashing red lights pulled up to the scene, and two officers jumped out to clear innocent bystanders out of the way. When they waved away the white smoke pouring out of the bonnet of the purple car, there were Pinky and Binky with their white mime faces planted firmly in the front-seat airbags. "I surrender!" shouted Sue from the back seat.

Spider-Man pulled himself up to his feet, dusted off the well-worn knees of his costume and walked over to the site of the crash. Everyone on the pavement stopped and stared. It was really him!

Because he spent his days at Midtown High School as honours student Peter Parker (or 'Pete the Science Geek', as the football team called him), Peter did most of his super hero work at night. This was the first time Peter had taken the Spidey suit out for a spin in broad daylight.

He walked down the street saluting and waving to the citizens of New York, the star of his own parade! But the crowd that should have been excited to see him instead whispered to each other and pointed at his back. One of the police officers noticed what they were seeing and called out to him. "Hey, Spider-Man! Wait!"

"No need to thank me, officer," Spider-Man said. "It's just another day at the office for Spider-Man!"

"No," the officer interrupted. "I mean...." Rather than finish his sentence, he politely twirled his finger to signal to the web-slinger to turn round.

At first, Spider-Man didn't notice the
giggling ladies snapping pictures behind
him. But then he felt the breeze on his
backside. The seat of his trousers had
been completely torn away and
his underpants were showing!
The whole crowd roared with
laughter! One by one, TV news
vans and reporters pulled
up. Spider-Man knew that
if he stuck around, his
boxer shorts would
be all over the six
o'clock news.

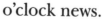

So with the push of a button on his web-shooter, he was out of sight in the blink of an eye. He was right. This was just another day for Spider-Man – filled with bad luck.

The next morning, at the office of the Daily Bugle newspaper, its infamous publisher, J. Jonah Jameson slammed his fist down on a pile of that day's newspapers. The New York Times, Daily News and New York Post all had the biggest story of the year on their front pages: the news of Spider-Man's daytime debut right in the middle of Times Square!

"Every paper in the city is all over this," Jonah said. "Every newspaper except for the Bugle! And we wonder why our circulation is in the toilet!"

"Everyone's circulation is in the toilet," said Bugle Editor-in-Chief Joe 'Robbie' Robertson as he stirred his coffee.

Robbie was as cool as Jonah was fiery. He learned years ago that for the Daily Bugle to be a success, it needed him to be the voice of reason whenever J.J.J. flew off the handle, and today was no exception.

"All the people we've got left were all downtown covering the Maggia trial," he said, taking a sip.

"Organized crime? That's yesterday's news, Robbie." Jonah jabbed a finger down on the newspapers. "Super heroes. Super villains. Weirdos with magical powers jumping around in their pyjamas. Costumed vigilantes operating outside of the law. Now there's some news!"

"But before yesterday, nobody'd ever got a good look at him," Robbie replied. "By the looks of these pictures, they still haven't. None of these pictures is showing anything but his goofy underpants!"

"New plan, effective immediately: our top priority is to get any and all pictures of this Spider-Man, using any means necessary," said Jonah.

"Uh-oh," Robbie leaned back in

his chair, cupping his coffee mug between his hands. "I've seen that look. You're up to no good."

"If Spider-Man wants to be famous," Jonah said, "we'll make him famous!"

CHAPTER

2

The Marshall Corporation on the Upper East Side of Manhattan is where the future is being made. At least, that's what the sign outside says. The truth is, the company hasn't made anything but a mess since old Mr Marshall retired and left his son, Albert, in charge.

Right from the start, Albert made steep budget cuts and moved most of the operations overseas. Those who were left in the New York factory were young, inexperienced and inexpensive. But the glue that held the company together was an old-timer named Adrian Toomes, who had been there so long he was practically furniture. Even though Mr Toomes taught the young engineers everything he knew, they made fun of his bald head and old-fashioned ways behind his back. Once they became good at their jobs, the young engineers often left for better opportunities, leaving their old teacher behind.

On this day, the five o'clock bell signalled the end of the workday just as it had thousands of times before for

Adrian Toomes, but this time it was different. Though Mr Toomes didn't know it yet, it was the last time he would ever hear it. After he said goodbye to the young engineers who were watching one of his demonstrations, he walked down the hall to his office to hang up his lab coat.

"Hello, Mr Toomes." Albert Marshall had been waiting for him, which was never a good sign. Albert didn't have a reputation for dropping by to give good news.

"Nice bird," he said, admiring the green parrot that stood on a perch in the corner. Mr Toomes was always interested in birds; he thought a bird in flight was Mother Nature's finest work of engineering. In fact, his office was decorated with bird pictures, statues and, for many years, his pet parrot, Menlo.

"What do you want, Albert?"

"Fine, Mr Toomes, I'll just get right to it," Albert said as he paced back and forth, picking the lint off of his fancy Italian suit.

"You've been with the Marshall Corp. for, what, ten ... twelve years?"

"Thirty-six," Mr Toomes said.

"Right," Albert said, not really caring. "Well, then you also know that for the past couple of years, business has been ... less than great. So I've decided to make some changes – for example, maybe replace some of our old equipment with some newer, younger models."

Mr Toomes was relieved. For a minute there, he thought he was getting fired.

"And that includes employees," Albert finished.

Mr Toomes' face dropped. "Wait," he said. "You're FIRING ME?!"

"SQUAWWK!" Menlo wailed, startling Albert so badly he nearly jumped right out of his shiny alligator shoes! He ducked down behind a chair.

"Mr Toomes, this company was founded on cutting-edge technology. Today, the competition is fierce. And you ... you haven't brought a worthwhile pitch to the floor since you had a full head of hair."

"But what about the Vulture?"

"The Vulture?" Albert asked, slowly standing up now that Menlo had calmed down. "You mean your ... bird suit?"

"It's not a bird suit. The Vulture is a harness that turns an average human being into a low-cost, eco-friendly aerial-assault weapon. The Department of Defence might have use for something like that."

Albert swallowed hard to hold down his laughter. "A harness?"

Mr Toomes flipped open his appointment book. "If you want, I can schedule a demonstration—"

"I'm sorry, Mr Toomes," Albert said, "but it has already been decided. You have one hour to pack up your things. Security will escort you out of the building." And with that, he walked to the door.

"Albert, wait!" Mr Toomes put his face down in his hands. "My retirement account was wiped out in the stock-market crash. This job is all I have. Please."

"You know, Dad always said you were the most resourceful man he knew," Albert said. "I'm sure you'll think of something."

Menlo the parrot flew off his perch in a rage, pecking and flapping his wings against Albert's head!

"SQUAWWWWK!"

Albert covered his head and ran
screaming down the hall!

"Let him go, Menlo," Mr Toomes
said. "It's my fault. All my life, I've let people
like him walk all over me. But never again!
I'm too old for that now. Albert's right, I
am resourceful ... and I know exactly what I
have to do. And finally everyone will know
that the Vulture is no laughing matter!"

Peter Parker zigzagged along the pavement, sidestepping children, briefcases and umbrella handles with ease. In the past, he'd have a hard time getting away from Flash Thompson and his bully buddies. But now that he had super-agility, it was all too easy. If he wanted, he could take on all of them with his super-strength and be sure they'd never bother him again, but he had to be very careful to keep his powers hidden so nobody would find out he was really Spider-Man. It was best to avoid confrontation completely.

The signal at the crossing said 'Don't Walk'. But with Flash and his buddies gaining on him, Peter took a deep breath and crossed the busy street, anyway. Flash was going to follow, but thought better of it when he got to the kerb. *Nobody in his right mind would ever run into that rush-hour traffic*, he thought. *Is Parker crazy?*

Then again, nobody had Peter Parker's super-agility either. He was home free!

"You can't run forever, Puny Parker!" Flash shouted.

Peter laughed as he closed the door to his building behind him, but his good mood didn't last very long when he saw the eviction notice taped to Aunt May's front door.

Peter knew Aunt May was going to have trouble paying the rent after Uncle Ben passed away, but he didn't realize how bad things already were. He never expected they might be thrown out of their home.

Peter ripped the notice from the door and crumpled it in his hand. Aunt May heard him come in and peeked out from the kitchen to greet him. She was her usual cheerful self, but now Peter wondered whether it was all just an act. What else had she been hiding from him?

"Peter?" she asked. But he didn't respond. Instead, he headed straight up the stairs to his room without a word.

"Peter, wait!" she said, catching up with him on the stairs. "Before you go up and disappear into your room, there's something important I need to tell you."

Peter held up his fist that had the crumpled-up eviction notice in it. "I already saw it," he said, and then started back up the stairs.

"No, not that," she said, stopping him again. Then she held up a camera.

"This. Our neighbour Willie Lumpkin thinks it might be worth something. It's an antique, but it has a self-timer. I found it in a box of things from Uncle Ben's wardrobe and—"

"WHAT?!" Peter shouted. He couldn't believe it! Uncle Ben had just passed away, and Aunt May was already selling his stuff! "Put it back! PUT IT ALL BACK!"

"Peter." Aunt May approached him gently. "I know you feel a lot of guilt over the way things ended with Uncle Ben. I do, too! I know what you're going through."

But she didn't know. She knew Peter and Uncle Ben had an argument before he died, but she didn't know Peter felt personally responsible for what happened to his uncle. "No, you don't. You can't!"

"Well, then tell me! Instead of staying out all day and locking yourself in your room all night, tell me so I can understand!"

"I—" Peter replied. "Just please don't sell his stuff!"

"But you didn't let me finish! In that same box, I found this." She held up a little brown leather notebook. "It's a bankbook from one of Uncle Ben's old accounts. I called the bank ... and it's still active. Peter, we have the rent money!"

Peter couldn't hold back any longer. At once, all of those tears he'd been holding in for so many days came pouring down his face. Aunt May hugged him tight around the neck.

"There, there," she said. "Everything's going to be all right from now on.
I promise."

CHAPTER
3

The Greater Community Bank of New York City's lobby was so big, the sound of the woman's tapping at her computer keyboard echoed high into the vaulted ceiling and fell down like rain all around Aunt May and Peter as they sat patiently in their seats. The sunlight coming in through the high glass walls shone on them brightly like a spotlight. Peter had brought Uncle Ben's old camera with him and he fiddled with it nervously.

When they were finished, he wanted to take some photos around the city and bring the film to the old camera shop in their neighbourhood to be developed and turned into a scrapbook.

On the subway ride to the bank, Aunt May had told Peter that years ago when Uncle Ben was in college, he had his own darkroom where he used a chemical solution and photo paper to develop his film into photographs. She said Peter could turn the upstairs bathroom into his own darkroom if he wanted to experiment. Aunt May knew Peter loved science and would never be able to resist such a project!

Between rounds of frantic typing that seemed to go on forever, the bank lady, Miss Maloney, glared at them over her glasses – and then pushed her glasses up the bridge of her nose and tapped at the keys again.

TAKKA TAKKA
TAK TAK TAKKA
TAKKA

"Is there a problem?" Aunt May
finally asked.

"Your husband didn't add you to this
account, Mrs Parker?"

"He's had it since before we
were married...."

Miss Maloney returned to her typing,
and then glared at Aunt May over her
glasses again. "It wasn't in his will?"
she asked.

"It isn't much without all of the interest
added in," Aunt May replied. "It must have
slipped his mind."

Miss Maloney removed her glasses and smiled. "I'm sorry, Mrs Parker," Miss Maloney said. "There's nothing I can do for you."

Aunt May sprang from her chair. "What?" Peter gently squeezed her hand to get her to sit back down again. "I mean ... there must be a way to...."

Miss Maloney leaned forward and crossed her hands on her desk like a stern schoolteacher. "Mrs Parker, bank policy states we'd need a signed and notarized letter from the account holder before letting you withdraw the funds."

This time, it was Peter who leaped from his chair. "That'd be kind of hard to get now, don't you think?!"

"Peter, please!" Aunt May grabbed his arm and pulled him back down. "Just go back to playing with your camera."

Peter couldn't believe Aunt May had dismissed him like that. He was the man of the house now. And a super hero, to boot! He could do whatever a spider could and spin a web of any size to catch thieves like flies! *If Aunt May only knew,* he thought to himself.

"Excuse me, Miss Maloney, but may I speak with a manager, please?" Aunt May asked calmly.

"Mrs Parker, I don't see how that will make any difference."

Aunt May started to lose her patience. "This is very urgent, so can you PLEASE GET ME A MANAGER?!" Miss Maloney scurried off to find one.

While they waited, Peter loaded a roll of film into the old camera and put it up to his eye. The zoom lens was out of focus, so he aimed at a faraway rooftop through the glass walls and noticed an odd, green figure. He slowly turned the lens to focus and saw it was an old man. An old man in a peculiar green costume with large wings! And with the old man's beak-like nose and bald head, he kind of looked like a bird.

Before Peter could show him to Aunt May, the man took a running start and jumped off the roof!

Peter put the camera down to see with his own eyes. There was the man, gliding across the busy street on those magnificent wings ... headed right for the bank!

KARRSCHCH!

When the Vulture crashed through the glass, shattering half the wall to pieces, Peter pulled Aunt May down to the floor behind the desk to cover her. Customers ran for the front door. Bank cashiers ducked behind the counter. The security guard closest to the intruder reached for his gun, but the Vulture grabbed him by the throat and lifted him high in the air before he could unholster it. He spun the guard around and threw him into another security guard who was sneaking over to help.

By the time the Vulture noticed the third security guard, his gun was already drawn. The guard fired three shots! But the Vulture shielded himself with one

of his wings, and the bullets bounced
off harmlessly. They were bulletproof!
Then, the Vulture thrust his arm towards
the guard. Several razor-sharp feathers
launched from the wing, hitting their target
with precision.

"A-all right," the Vulture said.
"Everyone stay calm. I don't want to
hurt anyone. Just stay where you are and
everything will be fine."

After he made sure Aunt May was all right, Peter told her to stay put and began to crawl away from their hiding place. "Peter, where are you going?" she whispered loudly, grabbing him by the shirt.

"I'm just ... going to get some pictures." But what Peter really had in mind was to find a place to stash Uncle Ben's old camera and change into the red and blue Spider-Man costume he had begun wearing under his clothes in case of emergencies like this one.

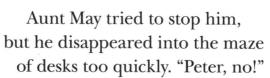

Aunt May tried to stop him, but he disappeared into the maze of desks too quickly. "Peter, no!"

"You!" The Vulture grabbed Miss Maloney by the shoulders and shook her. "Get a large bag and lead me to the vault!"

Then, as quick as a flash, Spider-Man swung across the room and kicked the Vulture on the side of the head, knocking him off his feet. Miss Maloney landed hard on the floor, but crawled safely into the corner.

"I don't believe my eyes!" Spider-Man said. "Just when I thought it couldn't get any weirder than a friendly neighbourhood Spider-Man, right here, as I live and breathe, is a bank-robbing buzzard!"

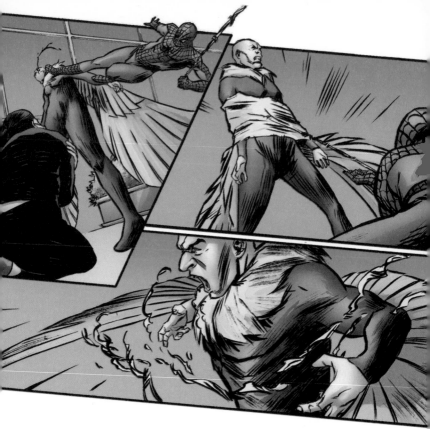

"The Spider-Man?" This was more
than the Vulture had expected on his first
outing as a super villain. Spider-Man aimed
both web-shooters at him and sprayed webs
around his body, wrapping him up around
the ribs like a mummy. But in the Vulture
suit, Adrian Toomes wasn't just an ordinary
old man; he was a lot stronger than
Spider-Man knew. He popped his sharp

wings out as hard as he could
against the webs that bound
him and they sliced through
the sticky webbing with ease.
He was free!

"This is not what
I wanted!" the Vulture
said. He jumped up,
flapping his
wings. Before
anyone knew
it, he was flying
higher and
higher towards
the ceiling.
Spider-Man
wasn't about to
let another
criminal get
away the
way he did
the night of
Uncle Ben's murder
and shot a web at his legs
to slow him down.

"Hey, it's not what I wanted either Buzzy," called Spider-Man. "But we don't have much of a choice now."

But instead of Spider-Man's web pulling the Vulture down, the power of the Vulture's wings pulled Spider-Man up! And up and up and up they went!

Then, once Miss Maloney saw it, she called out to him, "Hey, Spider-Man?"

But he didn't need to hear the rest of what she was going to say. He knew as soon as he felt the breeze on his backside. *Crud,* he thought to himself, *I didn't get a chance to fix my trousers.*

CHAPTER
4

The Vulture pulled Spider-Man so high, they crashed right through the glass ceiling of the Greater Community Bank ... and kept on going! But no matter how high they flew, Spider-Man still held on! The Vulture weaved in between buildings, turned sharply round corners, but Spider-Man still held on! He twisted and twirled in the air, climbed and fell sharply, but Spider-Man still held on! He used every trick his Vulture suit was capable of, but he just couldn't get Spider-Man off his tail!

Holding on to the web for dear life, Spider-Man realized he had made the wrong choice again. He had no real plan for how to stop the Vulture aside from holding on to that web with all of his might! It was just like when he was dragged by Pinky, Binky and Sue's purple car. *That's it!* he thought, *I know what I have to do!*

While holding on to his web with one hand, he reached out with his other and fired a web at a nearby building. It stuck! And with a web held firmly in each hand – one attached to the building and the other to the Vulture's leg – he pulled Toomes to an abrupt stop in mid-air!

Then, Spider-Man yanked the Vulture back to him and they grappled in the air as they tumbled towards the streets below! "Nice outfit," Spider-Man said. "Is today your day off from greeting customers outside of Frank's Chicken Hut, grandpa?"

"You underestimate me, spider-boy!" Toomes replied. "The Vulture harness doesn't just give me the ability to fly, it gives me the strength of 20 men!"

Though the Vulture had a good grip on him, Spider-Man was able to wrestle his arm free. "Congratulations. But let's see how you do FLYING BLIND!" With the push of a button, the web-shooter shot

THWIP!

a sticky blob of webbing right across the
Vulture's eyes, covering them like a mask.

The Vulture grabbed at his face,
trying to peel it off. Without his sight, he
was no match for anyone! He tried to fly
away, but this time Spider-Man learned
from his mistake. With a hard tug on the
web, he vaulted himself right onto the
Vulture's back!

"You're not good at this at all,"
Spider-Man said. "Maybe you'd better
let me steer for a while."

He held the webs like reins, pulling the
Vulture this way and that. The Vulture tried
to wriggle free, but couldn't. While they
fought over control, they suddenly realized
they were headed straight for a skyscraper.

"Let go!" the Vulture screamed. "You'll
kill us both!"

"Okay, have it your way!" When
Spider-Man let go of the reins, he gave
the Vulture one last shove to send
him crashing through a window!

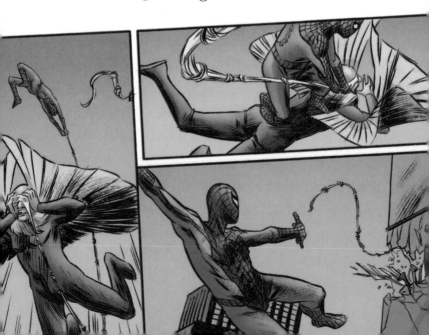

Spider-Man crawled through the window to make sure Toomes didn't get away and found the injured old man lying in a pile of broken glass and furniture. The harness may have given him extraordinary abilities, but Adrian Toomes was still just a man in a bird suit who was in way over his head.

"Serves you right for flying without a licence," Spider-Man quipped as he carefully webbed up his foe's arms and wings tightly so there'd be no escape this time.

Spider-Man carried him out of the wreckage and gently lowered him to the ground, where two police officers were waiting to take him away.

"You're just a kid," Toomes said to Spider-Man. "You don't know what it's like to be all alone. To be out of money. I had no choice."

"That's where you're wrong," Spider-Man said. As Peter Parker, he and Aunt May were about to get kicked out of their apartment because they didn't have rent money.

"We can't always control the things that happen to us, but how we react to them is always our choice." The police officers tipped their caps to Spider-Man and led the Vulture to their squad car.

"I CAN'T BELIEVE IT!" a man shouted from behind.

"I know, I know," Spider-Man said. "I didn't get a chance to fix my trousers."

"It's you! Spider-Man! Right here in front of me! And this stupid battery's dead on my camera! I could have finally paid off my student loans! Stupid! Stupid! Stupid!"

Spider-Man saw the man with a goatee and baseball cap shaking his camera and asked, "What are you talking about?"

The man pulled a sheet of folded paper from his back pocket and handed it to him. "You don't know? These are all over the city."

It was a flier with the Daily Bugle logo at the top and a picture of its famous publisher, J. Jonah Jameson, pointing like Uncle Sam in an Army recruitment poster.

Beneath the image it read, 'The Daily Bugle
Wants You! Cash reward for best photos of
Spider-Man!'. And suddenly, Peter had an
idea of how to save the apartment.

"These pictures are amazing! It looks
like he's actually posing for you!"

In all their years together at the
Daily Bugle, Robbie Robertson had never

seen J. Jonah Jameson so excited over
pictures and knew at once they had found
their winner. "How did you get these?"
Jonah asked, as Robbie motioned for the
other aspiring photographers to leave.

Peter Parker just shrugged his
shoulders. "I don't know, sir. Just lucky,
I guess." Of course, Peter couldn't tell
him the truth – he did pose for them!

"Poppycock!" Jonah shouted.
"You make your own luck through hard
work, Porter."

"His name's Parker," Robbie said
with bemusement and placed a proud
hand on young Peter's shoulder.

Jonah slammed the stack
of photos down and walked
out from behind his desk.

He pulled Peter away from Robbie, and with an arm around his neck, he said to him in a very un-Jonah-like soft voice, "Forget the reward. How would you like to work for me?"

"Jonah! He's just a kid," Robbie said, not liking the idea at all.

"Freelance! For cash! What do you say, kid?" It was out of Robbie's hands. Jonah and Peter both had the look on their faces that said they were up to no good.

And from that day on, Peter Parker was the Daily Bugle's anonymous staff photographer by day and patrolled the streets of New York City as a super hero by night. When danger called, he simply climbed a nearby wall, webbed the camera to it and set its automatic timer to catch himself in action. The next day, he'd deliver the pictures to Jonah and bring the money home to pay Aunt May's rent!

It turned out Willie Lumpkin was right – that old camera was worth something.

"And now, here's a brief demonstration of how we experiment with radioactivity here in the lab." Dr Lee, a physicist at Empire State University, motioned to

Mr Ditko, head of Midtown High's science department, to push a button on the console in front of him. The room full of students 'oohed' and 'ahhed' as a cluster of large machines behind the safety glass beeped and buzzed with colourful lights.

"The ionization of atoms is known to cause cancer in living cells," Dr Lee said. "Hence the six-inch glass separating us from the equipment." The scientist flipped a switch and the largest machine in the room roared to life. An electrical beam zapped from one contact to the other, covering the room in a glow of blue light. Dr Lee pressed more buttons and the blue electricity crackled loudly as the two contacts on the machine moved closer together. "But it's also been known to cause anomalies in them as well."

Usually, a scientific demonstration this remarkable would easily grab Peter Parker's attention, but he wasn't in the mood today. His glasses broke in the scuffle outside, so he couldn't see very well anyway, but mostly, he felt bad for yelling at Uncle Ben.

He wasn't angry with him, but he was really angry at himself for letting Flash humiliate him. And every time he tried to forget about it, he heard the whispers from the back of the room.

"That old man better not say a word to my mum," said Flash. "If I get grounded and miss the game this weekend, I'll take it out on Puny Parker for the rest of the year!"

As Dr Lee lectured, a small spider lowered itself from its web down into the energy beam between the crackling contacts. Once the beams hit it, the spider jumped wildly! It kicked its legs back and forth, but couldn't wriggle free. The blue light crackled louder and brighter.

"We experiment with bacteria, fungi, insects and arachnids ..." Dr Lee continued, "... trying to create anomalies here in the lab so we can study them to find out why they occur so that we can learn to control them."

"I say we give him a warning shot now," Flash said from the back of the room, "so he knows I mean business."

Suddenly, the lights on the control panel flickered red. The machines roared louder.

"Wait, something seems to be—" Dr Lee began, but the control panel exploded in a shower of sparks! The machines began to smoke!

"Everyone get back!" Dr Lee shouted. The light flared so brightly, the students shielded their eyes.

"Come on, guys, let's get out of here," Flash shouted and pushed the door open. Mr Ditko ordered the whole class to follow him out to the car park, but Peter was mesmerized by what was happening. This was real science!

Suddenly – SKRASSH! – the machine behind the window exploded, spraying the room with a million pieces of glass! Peter put his arms in front of his face to protect himself, but he felt a sharp pinch in the back of his hand. Broken glass! "OWWW!" he shrieked.

Except it wasn't. Peter looked at his hand and saw the little black spider that soaked up all of the radiation in the experiment. It must have been thrown by the explosion and, in desperation, bit into the first thing that it landed on.

"Son, are you okay?" Dr Lee asked as he pulled Peter outside by the arm. Peter watched the spider stiffen and fall dead to the floor.

"Come ON!" Dr Lee shouted.

"Class, stay together while we call the paramedics," Mr Ditko said, but as his classmates gathered on the pavement, Peter kept walking.

He wasn't feeling well; he was dizzy and his legs felt rubbery. "Hey, wait!" Mr Ditko shouted. "You can't leave until we make sure you're all right!"

But Peter wouldn't listen. His stomach was in knots. The spider bite on his hand throbbed. He needed to get away.

"Hey, Flash, where's Puny Parker going?" one of the bullies whispered.

"Nowhere we can't get to him. Come on," Flash said.

Across the street, Peter escaped into

a secluded alley lined with bins. He felt sick to his stomach and couldn't hold it anymore! He grabbed the lid off one of the bins and ... "BLARRGGHH!"

What's happening? he wondered. *Am I allergic to spider bites...?*